SUSAN PEARSON

The Day Po... Climbed the Christmas Tree

ILLUSTRATED BY RICK BROWN

SIMON AND SCHUSTER BOOKS FOR YOUNG READERS

PUBLISHED BY SIMON & SCHUSTER INC., NEW YORK

Simon and Schuster Books for Young Readers, Simon and Schuster Building,
Rockefeller Center, 1230 Avenue of the Americas, New York, New York 10020.
Text Copyright © 1987 by Susan Pearson. Illustrations copyright © 1987 by Rick
Brown. All rights reserved including the right of reproduction in whole or in part in
any form. SIMON AND SCHUSTER BOOKS FOR YOUNG READERS is a trademark of
Simon & Schuster Inc. Manufactured in the United States of America.

10 9 8 7 6 5 4 3 2 1 (pbk)   10 9 8 7 6 5 4 3 2 1

Library of Congress Cataloging-in-Publication Data. Pearson, Susan. The day
Porkchop climbed the christmas tree. Summary: A rambunctious kitten named
Porkchop climbs the Christmas tree and gives a brother and sister their funniest
and most unforgettable Christmas ever. [1. Cats—Fiction. 2. Christmas—Fiction]
I. Brown, Rick, 1946-ill. II. Title. PZ7.P323316 Day 1987 [E] 87-2532

ISBN 0-13-197559-5; ISBN 0-671-68884-7 (pbk.)

The Day Porkchop Climbed the Christmas Tree

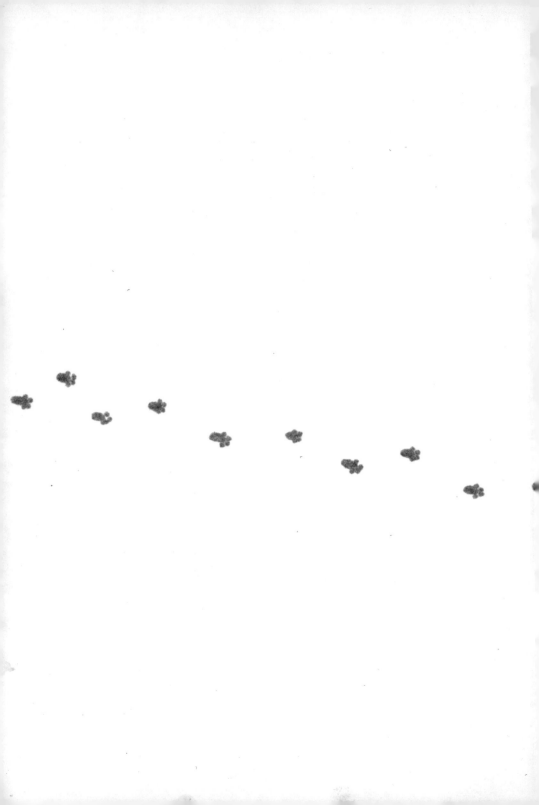

Chapter 1

PORKCHOP IN COLD WATER

I say it all started with Rosie's birthday.

Rosie says, "It did not, Nicky! It started with the Christmas cookies!"

Dad says we're both wrong. It started with the icicles.

Mom says, "Who cares when it started? I'm just glad it ended!"

We all know when that was. The day Porkchop climbed the tree.

Porkchop is Rosie's kitten. She got him for her birthday.

"Porchops come from *pigs*," I told her, "not cats."

"Who cares," said Rosie. "Catchop sounds stupid."

"He'll turn out weird," I warned her.

I was right. First off, Porkchop was crazy about snow.

"At least he's easy to please," said Mom.

Already we'd had seven snow days, and it was only December 1. On sunny days, the icicles hanging down from our roof sparkled like diamonds.

"Wow!" I said. "We live in an ice castle!"

"Hmph," said Dad. "As soon as it warms up, the roof will leak. A January thaw will turn this house into a swimming pool."

We didn't get a January thaw. We got a December thaw.

Dad was right about the roof. It leaked, all right. It leaked in the living room. It leaked in the hall. It leaked over the stairs. It leaked in my bedroom. We were running out of buckets.

Every night we went to sleep to *plunk plunk plunk*.

Every morning we woke up to *splash splash splash*.

I liked falling asleep to the drips. Rosie was jealous because her room didn't leak. Porkchop was just plain in heaven. It figured. A cat who loved snow was bound to like water.

All day long he raced from bucket to bucket. I think he knocked the first one over by mistake. After that, I'm pretty sure it was on purpose.

The thaw only lasted a few days. Then it turned cold again, and the roof stopped leaking. Dad felt better. Then it started to snow. Dad felt worse.

"I don't know where to put it anymore," he groaned.

Every night was the same. Dad came home from work. He changed his clothes. Then he climbed up on the roof to push off the snow.

Monday Rosie and I used it to build a snow fort.

Tuesday we loaded it in laundry baskets and carried it to the curb.

Wednesday Dad got a cold and went to bed. Mom made him a cup of hot cider. Porkchop drank it while Dad was putting on his pajamas.

Chapter 2

PORKCHOP CHOPS

On Friday Mom began the Christmas baking. Usually she loves to do it, but this year there was Porkchop.

On Saturday he knocked over a whole tray of rosettes. They smashed into a million pieces.

On Sunday he spilled powdered sugar all over the floor.

On Monday afternoon he walked across two cookie sheets of gingerbread men. He left a paw print in every one. Then he climbed into the oven.

"Rosemary Sarah!" Mom hollered. "If you don't get this cat out of the kitchen, you'll be eating Porkchop chops for dinner!"

We always trim our tree on December 17. On December 18, we have a party. December 18 is Mom's birthday.

On December 17, it was my turn to do the dishes. I turned on the tap. Nothing happened. Then Rosie tried. Then Mom tried. Still nothing.

"The pipes must have frozen," said Dad.

"Not tonight!" Mom groaned.

Rosie turned the tap back on. "Maybe we'll get ice cubes," she said.

Just then Porkchop skidded into the kitchen, screeched to a stop under the table, and sneezed a cloud of black dust. Black paw prints covered the kitchen floor.

"I guess I left the fireplace screen open," Dad confessed.

"Grab that cat!" Mom shouted.

Rosie dove under the table, but she was too slow. Porkchop hightailed it out of the kitchen like a miniature black locomotive.

"After him!" Dad shouted.

The chase was on. Through the dining room. Through the living room. Behind the couch. Over the chairs. Under the piano. Up the hallway. Down

the hallway. Into the bathroom.

I slammed the door shut. Porkchop was trapped inside.

Then Mom took over. She sent Dad to the roof.
It was snowing again. She sent Rosie next door to
borrow a heater for the pipes. She sent me to the store
to buy paper plates.

When we got home, she was sitting on the floor,
looking at the empty tree, crying.

It all worked out. Rosie cleaned Porkchop up with snow. He loved that. Dad cleaned up all the paw prints. The tree got trimmed.

The party was great. No one cared about the paper plates. We were too busy singing. And the pipes finally unfroze with a big bang right in the middle of "Silent Night."

Chapter 3

MERRY CHRISTMAS, PORKCHOP!

Then nothing bad happened for two days. It stopped snowing. Nothing leaked. Porkchop stayed out of trouble.

"Something is not right," said Mom.

"It's the calm before the storm," said Dad.

I figured Porkchop had been so bad all week, he needed a rest.

The Saturday before Christmas, we all went downtown. Except for Porkchop, of course. We did some Christmas shopping. We took Rosie to see Santa Claus. We walked around looking at all the decorations. It was getting dark when we got home.

Mom opened the front door. She turned on the light. Then she screamed.

We all ran in behind her. We looked where she was looking. There was Porkchop, halfway up the tree.

The decorations were rattling. The angel was tottering. The tinsel was jiggling like Jell-O. The tree was swaying.

Up he climbed, higher and higher. And the higher he climbed, the more the tree swayed. We all just stood there watching it. I guess none of us knew what to do.

Porkchop was getting close to the top. It bent down under his weight. The angel fell to the floor. Porkchop leaped after her. And then, ever so slowly, the tree followed them down.

I thought Mom would cry. I thought Dad would yell. But for five minutes no one said anything. No one moved.

Then Mom started to laugh. Then Dad started to laugh. I looked at Rosie. Rosie looked at me.

"It must be okay," I told her, and we laughed too.

"You build a fire," Mom told Dad. "And you two change clothes," she said to Rosie and me. "Put on something extra nice."

"This is it," I whispered to Rosie. "Mom has flipped!"

But we did as we were told.

When we came back all dressed up, the tree was still on the floor. The tree lights were on, though. All the others were off.

There was a fire in the fireplace. There was a plate of cookies on the floor, and a jug of cocoa, and *five* cups. One was for Porkchop, I guessed.

There was also a bowl of popcorn. Porkchop was eating that, but no one seemed to care.

Mom was in her best dress. Dad was in his best suit. Shopping bags were all over the place.

"Merry Christmas, Nick," said Mom. She handed me a bag.

"Merry Christmas, Rosie." She handed Rosie a bag.

"Merry Christmas, Richard." She handed Dad a bag.

"And Merry Christmas, Porkchop!" She tossed him a catnip mouse.

We had popcorn and cookies for dinner that night. And we opened all our presents. Well, not exactly opened. We took them out of the bags.

I thought that might make Christmas Day a little sad. It didn't.

On Christmas morning we sat around the tree. Dad had put it back up again. It was missing a few balls, but no one cared.

We sang some Chrismas carols. Then we told some stories. Some were about Rosie and me when we were little. Some were about Mom and Dad before Rosie and I were born. And some, of course, were about Porkchop.

I think it was the nicest Christmas I ever had.